# What's So Special About This Fall?

# I'M GOING TO SCHOOL

by Jane Belk Moncure
illustrated by Jenny Williams

Created by

THE CHILD'S WORLD

Distributed by CHILDRENS PRESS®
Chicago, Illinois

CHILDRENS PRESS HARDCOVER EDITION
ISBN 0-516-05712-X

CHILDRENS PRESS PAPERBACK EDITION
ISBN 0-516-45712-8

**Library of Congress Cataloging in Publication Data**

Moncure, Jane Belk.
  What's so special about this fall? : I'm going
to school / by Jane Belk Moncure
  (What's so special)

  Summary: A child describes first-day-at-school
experiences, including meeting Squeaky the guinea pig,
playing with blocks, snack and rest time, and
visiting the playground.
  [1. Schools—Fiction]   I. Williams, Jenny, ,
1939-        ill.   II. Title.   III. Series.
PZ7.M739Whgb   1988          [E]          88-2868
ISBN 0-89565-420-2

1 2 3 4 5 6 7 8 9 10 11 12 R 96 95 94 93 92 91 90 89 88

# What's So Special About This Fall?

# I'M GOING TO SCHOOL

What's so special about this fall?
I'm going to school, that's what.
Today is the first day, and I'm
ready to go.

But I'm glad my mom is going
with me.

Last week we came here to
"open house," so we know
where we're going.

My room is the one with the
clown on the door.

I met my teacher, Mrs. Michael,
at open house. She's pretty, and
she smiles a lot.

I have a special place to keep
my things. Billy has a place
next to mine.

First, we have "circle time." I
sit next to Billy. Mrs. Michael
has a surprise.

It's a guinea pig. His name is
Squeaky. This is his first day
at school too.

"If he likes it here, he will
whistle for you," says Mrs.
Michael.

We talk about how we can get
Squeaky to whistle by feeding
him and being kind to him.

"If we are kind to each other too,"
says Mrs. Michael, "maybe all of
us will want to whistle by the end
of the day."

Next it is work time. Squeaky
watches us. We can choose things
to do. Some of us work puzzles,
some of us play games, and some
look at books.

Some children play store. Others
color or work with clay.

Billy and I choose building blocks.

Next we have music time. I play the cymbals. Billy plays the drum.

We march around Squeaky's cage, but Squeaky doesn't whistle yet.

After snack time and rest time,
we make a long train. We go
clickety—clack down the track . . .

all the way to the playground.
We swing . . .

and race and play kick
ball.

But I like the climbing bars
best of all.

When we come inside, we play
a traffic-light game. I get to be
the traffic light. Everyone else
drives a car. When I hold up the
red light, everyone stops.

When I hold up the green light,
everyone goes fast. It's fun,
and we laugh a lot.

We make our own traffic-light
puppets to take home. One side
says, "Stop." One side says,
"Go." Mrs. Michael says we will
learn a lot of words this year.

I show my traffic-light puppet
to Squeaky, but he doesn't
whistle—not yet.

Before we go home, we have story
time. Mrs. Michael lets Squeaky sit
with us. While we are listening,
guess what happens? Squeaky whistles.
He really does!

"I think Squeaky likes our school,"
says Mrs. Michael.

Now it is time to say good-bye for
today. I try to whistle too . . .

. . . all the way home.